Tito, the Firefighter

written by / escrito por
Tim Hoppey

illustrated by / ilustrado por
Kimberly Hoffman

translated by / traducido por
Eida de la Vega

Tito, el Bombero

For Luis Cruz
–Tim Hoppey

For my husband and newborn daugher
–Kimberly Hoffman

Hoppey, Tim.

Tito, the firefighter = Tito, el bombero / written by Tim Hoppey = escrito por Tim Hoppey ; illustrated by Kimberly Hoffman = ilustrado por Kimberly Hoffman ; translated by Eida de la Vega = traducción por Eida de la Vega -- 1st ed. -- Green Bay, WI : Raven Tree Press, 2005.

p. ; cm.

Audience: ages 4-8.
Text in English with intermittent Spanish words. Summary: Tito admires his neighborhood bomberos (firefighters) and dreams of being a bombero himself. One day his ability to speak both English and Spanish actually helps the firefighters save the day.
ISBN: 0-9724973-3-1

1. Fire fighters--Juvenile fiction. 2. Fire extinction--Juvenile fiction.
3. Communication--Juvenile fiction. 4. Bilingual books.
5. [Spanish language materials--bilingual.] I. Hoffman, Kimberly, illus. II. Title.
III. Title: Tito, el bombero.

Printed in the U.S.A.

PZ7 .H677 2005   10987654321   2003092222
[E]--dc21   first edition   0501

Tito, the Firefighter

written by / escrito por
Tim Hoppey

illustrated by / ilustrado por
Kimberly Hoffman

translated by / traducido por
Eida de la Vega

Tito, el Bombero

Raven Tree Press LLC
www.raventreepress.com

Hello. *Hola.*
My name is Tito.

I live in East Harlem where almost everyone speaks Spanish.

When my mother sends
me to the store for milk and eggs,
I ask for *leche y huevos*.

If you ask how old I am,
I might say eight in
English. Or I might say
ocho in Spanish.

I am bilingual.
I speak two languages,
inglés and *español*.

This is Richie. He is a **bombero**.
I really want to ride in **el camión
de bomberos**. Richie says only
firefighters can ride in the fire truck.

Every morning I walk past
the firehouse. Richie yells,
    "Hola, Tito!"
"Hello" is one of the only
Spanish words he knows.

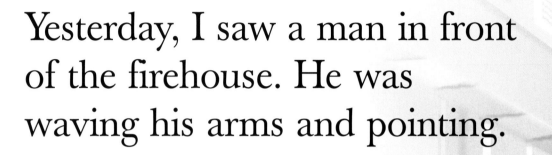

Yesterday, I saw a man in front of the firehouse. He was waving his arms and pointing.

I could tell something was very wrong. Something was *muy mal*.

Richie could tell that the man needed help. But he could not understand the man's *español*.

I ran over and spoke *inglés* for the man.

A smoke detector was ringing in the man's building. He thought he smelled smoke!

Richie rang the bells three times. Ringing the bells *tres* times means there is an emergency.

The *bomberos* all came running.

The **bomberos** put on their gear.
They climbed up on **el camión
de bomberos**.

Richie said, "Hop on, Tito.
We may need your help."

The fire truck raced down the street. The horn and siren were loud. The horn and **la sirena** sent out a message.

Look out! *¡Tenga cuidado!*

We raced past
the man who had
told us about the fire.

"Hurry! *¡Apúrense!*",
he shouted.

Richie asked me, "Which building is it, Tito?"
"¡El rojo!" I said.

Richie yelled, "In English, Tito! In English!"
"The red one! The man told me it was
the red one!" I yelled.

There was NOT a fire in the building. There was no *fuego* at all.

A woman fell asleep and took a *siesta* while cooking. She burned a pot of rice.

Still, it was exciting. The old men playing dominoes pointed at me and cheered when I climbed out of **el camión de bomberos**.

"Thanks for the help. **Gracias**," said Richie. "You're welcome. **De nada**," I said.

Because I am bilingual I got to be a ***bombero*** for a day.

Now when I walk past the firehouse I yell to Richie, *"**Hola, bombero!**"*

Richie yells back, *"**Hola**,* Tito, our little ***bombero**!"*

Vocabulario / Vocabulary

hola	hello
leche y huevos	milk and eggs
inglés	English
español	Spanish
ocho	eight
el bombero	firefighter
el camión de bomberos	fire truck
muy mal	very wrong
tres	three
la sirena	siren
tenga cuidado	look out
apúrense	hurry
la siesta	nap
el rojo	red
el fuego	fire
gracias	thank you
de nada	you're welcome